Dear Parents:

Congratulations! Your child is taking the first steps on an exciting journey. The destination? Independent reading!

STEP INTO READING® will help your child get there. The program offers five steps to reading success. Each step includes fun stories and colorful art or photographs. In addition to original fiction and books with favorite characters, there are Step into Reading Non-Fiction Readers, Phonics Readers and Boxed Sets, Sticker Readers, and Comic Readers—a complete literacy program with something to interest every child.

Learning to Read, Step by Step!

Ready to Read   Preschool–Kindergarten
• big type and easy words • rhyme and rhythm • picture clues
For children who know the alphabet and are eager to begin reading.

Reading with Help   Preschool–Grade 1
• basic vocabulary • short sentences • simple stories
For children who recognize familiar words and sound out new words with help.

Reading on Your Own   Grades 1–3
• engaging characters • easy-to-follow plots • popular topics
For children who are ready to read on their own.

Reading Paragraphs   Grades 2–3
• challenging vocabulary • short paragraphs • exciting stories
For newly independent readers who read simple sentences with confidence.

Ready for Chapters   Grades 2–4
• chapters • longer paragraphs • full-color art
For children who want to take the plunge into chapter books but still like colorful pictures.

STEP INTO READING® is designed to give every child a successful reading experience. The grade levels are only guides; children will progress through the steps at their own speed, developing confidence in their reading. The F&P Text Level on the back cover serves as another tool to help you choose the right book for your child.

Remember, a lifetime love of reading starts with a single step!

TM & copyright © by Dr. Seuss Enterprises, L.P. 2024

All rights reserved. Published in the United States by Random House Children's Books, a division of Penguin Random House LLC, New York. Featuring characters from *The Sneetches and Other Stories,* TM & copyright © 1961, and copyright renewed 1989 by Dr. Seuss Enterprises, L.P.

Step into Reading, Random House, and the Random House colophon are registered trademarks of Penguin Random House LLC.

Visit us on the Web!
Seussville.com
StepIntoReading.com
rhcbooks.com

Educators and librarians, for a variety of teaching tools, visit us at RHTeachersLibrarians.com

Library of Congress Cataloging-in-Publication Data is available upon request.
ISBN 978-0-593-70623-7 (trade) — ISBN 978-0-593-70624-4 (lib. bdg.)

Printed in the United States of America
10 9 8 7 6 5 4 3 2 1
First Edition

This book has been officially leveled by using the F&P Text Level Gradient™ Leveling System.

COOKING with the SNEETCHES

by Astrid Holm

illustrated by Erik Doescher

Random House 🏠 New York

What do Sneetches do on beaches?

Sneetches swim.
Sneetches play.

They read.

They walk.

They talk all day.

And when the sun
begins to go down,
they make a fire
and gather around.

Then Sneetches do
what they like most.

They have a
Sneetch Beach Hot Dog
Roast!

Each hot dog
goes on a stick.

Careful! Careful!
That's the trick!

Sizzle! Sizzle!

The hot dogs are done.

Now each one goes
inside a bun.

Some add mustard.

Some do not.

They eat the dogs
while they are hot.

Then the Sneetches take
a little rest . . .

. . . before they cook
what they LOVE best.

MARSHMALLOWS!

Roasted and toasted
with a golden crust,
marshmallows are
a Sneetch Beach Must!

And when stars begin
to light the sky,

the Sneetches will
then say goodbye.

And together they
will leave the beach . . .

. . . with sticky hands held

Sneetch to Sneetch.